# Timmy
# and Tiger

# Special Words

Special words help make this story fun.
Your child may need help reading them.

animal

door

eyes

food

Tiger

# Timmy and Tiger

Written by Mary Hooper
Illustrated by Lucy Su

Hooked On Phonics

**Hooked On Phonics**

# Contents

# 1. What's in That Bush?

Luke kicked the ball, and it shot past Timmy. It went under one of the bushes by the fence.

"Goal!" Luke yelled, leaping up and down.

"OK," Timmy said. "You win." And he went to find the ball.

"I am soaked, and I am going home!" Luke yelled. It had been raining. "See you next time!"

Timmy did not hear Luke. Something was in one of the bushes.

"Can't you find the ball?"
Luke called.

"I think a wild animal is in here!" Timmy said.

"Really?" Luke said.

"I think so," Timmy said.

"I am going home," Luke called.

Then Timmy saw something.

"Hi," he said softly.

Two eyes looked back at him. It was a lost cat. The cat backed deeper into the bush.

"It's OK. I will not hurt you!" Timmy said. "You can come home with me. I will give you some food!"

The cat gave a soft meow.

"Here, kitty, kitty. You can have a nice bowl of milk. And some of Duke's dog food, OK?"

It was dark under the bush.

"Duke is Pete's dog," Timmy said softly. "He's good. He will not hurt you."

He put his hand out to the cat.

"I bet you are lost," he said. His fingers petted the cat's fur. "You come home with me."

As he talked, Timmy reached for the cat. Grasping it gently, he backed out of the bush.

He got up with the cold, shivering cat in his arms.

"You are soaking!" he said.
He put the cat in the bottom of
his shirt.

"I am going to look after you!" said Timmy. "And even if you do not look much like one, I am going to call you Tiger."

# 2. Safe for Now

"I'll fix you up," Timmy whispered
to Tiger. "I'll get you some food
and make you a bed. And maybe I
can keep you." But he knew that
he couldn't keep Tiger.

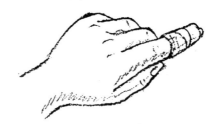

Timmy loved animals, but he had taken home too many animals in the past. There had been a hamster  and a rat that had gotten into the kitchen. And then there had been a rabbit that had eaten the flowers in the garden.

It was not very likely that
Timmy's mom was going to let
him keep Tiger....

As they went into the backdoor
of Timmy's house, Tiger was still
hidden in his big shirt.

"Now, just stay still," Timmy
whispered.

"Timmy! Look at your shirt!"

Timmy was on the porch with his ball under his arm and a big lump in his shirt.

"Take your shoes off!" his mom said. "Toss that ball outside. Then go upstairs and get in the tub."

Duke got up from his basket by the heater and padded up to Timmy. He could smell the cat.

"Go!" Timmy said, trying to get his sneakers off without squishing Tiger.

"I could see you from the window," Mom said. "Why were you boys playing in the rain?"

"We don't care if it's raining,"
Timmy said.
He went into the kitchen.

He held onto Tiger with one hand
and backed Duke off with the
other. He'd nearly made it when...

"Your shirt looks like a mess," Mom said.

"It's muddy," Timmy said. "I'll clean it."

"What?!" his mom said in surprise. "When have you ever...?"

But by then Timmy was leaping up the stairs two at a time.

Safe in his room, he put Tiger down.

"Bet you have not had a good meal for weeks," Timmy said. "Hope you like dog food."

Timmy patted Tiger dry, then put him on the bed and put the blanket over him.

"Stay here," he said. "I'm hungry too. I'm going to look for some food in the kitchen."

Tiger gave a short meow, then put his head down.

# 3. Time to Eat

"Did you have your bath yet?"
Mom asked.

"I will," Timmy
said. "But I
am hungry."

"Supper is any time now," Mom said, "so do not eat too much!"

"Just a glass of milk," Timmy said. He was hoping to see a can of dog food too.

There was no dog food.

Timmy put some milk into a glass. He was thinking, "I can share my milk with Tiger."

"What are we having for supper?" asked Timmy.

"Hot dogs and beans."

Hot dogs! Cats like hot dogs!

"Do you need help?" he asked.

"No, thanks," Mom said. "Just go and get in the tub!"

Just then, Timmy's mom looked out the window.

Timmy grabbed for a hot dog to take to Tiger.

"Put that back!" said his mom. "Get upstairs. I do not want to see you again until you are clean!"

Timmy went upstairs and started looking for something to put the milk in. "I will get you some food as fast as I can," he said to Tiger. "Maybe some of Duke's food, or a hot dog. Do you like hot dogs? I could go buy you a can of cat food or..."

Timmy did not hear the door opening. There was a yell, and then Mom said, "What is that cat doing on your bed?!"

# 4. No More Pets!

Timmy said Tiger was lost and hungry. But Mom stopped him.

"No, I'm sorry, Timmy. We can't have one more pet in the house." She picked Tiger up off the bed.

"He looks so sad because he's been sleeping outside!" Timmy said.

"That is sad," said Mom.

"He just needs care and food," Timmy said.

Mom sat down on the bed. Tiger came over to Timmy, rubbing himself on Timmy's leg.

"Oh, please let me keep him, Mom!" he said. "Pete's got Duke, but I do not have a pet!"

"No," said Mom, "we just can't pay for the cat's food."

"He can eat leftovers!"

"No, Timmy. He has to have real cat food and milk, and there would be shots and vet bills. No, you better say good-bye to the cat now, before you get too fond of him."

"I'm fond of him now," Timmy said. Timmy felt there was something good about Tiger, that he wasn't just any cat.

"Can I keep him for two weeks?"

"No, Timmy."

"A week, then."

"No!"

"A day. What does a day matter?" Timmy begged.

"It's best if…"

"Oh, Mom!" Timmy's eyes filled with tears.

His mom said, "OK, one day then. But after school he goes to the animal shelter."

Timmy sniffed back tears.

"The cat has to come downstairs and sleep in the kitchen. I do not want it up here with all its fleas."

Timmy did not think Tiger had fleas, but he was not going to say that to Mom.

"I will fix up a box by the heater," he said. "And, Mom, can he have a hot dog to eat?"

# 5. What Is It?

By supper time Tiger had had two hot dogs, some dog food, and a big dish of milk.

When Pete came in, Tiger was sitting near Duke's basket in the kitchen.

Pete looked at the cat. "What's that?"

"That's my cat," Timmy said.
"That's not a cat!" Pete said.
"It's a scrub brush on legs."
"He's not!" Timmy said. "Tiger is
a fantastic cat."

"Tiger!" Pete said. "I have never seen anything that looks less like a tiger."

Timmy looked at Pete's dog. "Well, he doesn't look like a duke!"

Duke looked at Tiger. Tiger looked at Duke. Duke shut his eyes.

"My Tiger's not scared of your silly dog!" Timmy said. "My Tiger's a supercat, he's..."

"Stop that," Mom said. "Go and wash your hands before we eat. And Timmy, do not think of that cat as yours because it's not."

"OK," Timmy muttered. "But what if I...?"

"No!" Mom said. "Don't even ask."

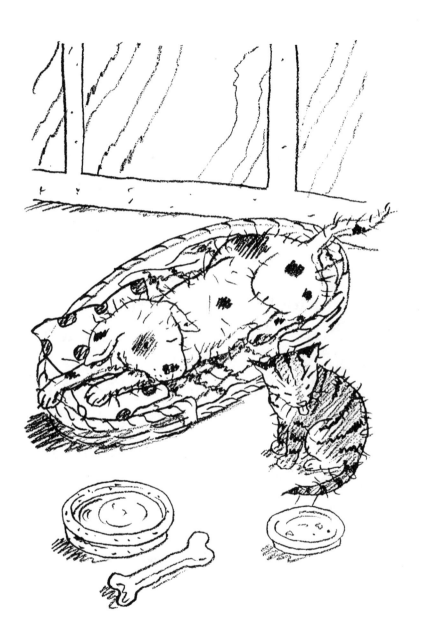

At bedtime Timmy got a box and put it next to the heater in the kitchen. He moved Duke's basket and got Tiger's box as close to the heater as he could.

"You feel better now, don't you?" he whispered. "And, when I take you down to the animal shelter..." Just then Timmy felt all choked up. "Mom, what do they do with cats at the animal shelter?" he asked.

"They find them good homes,"
Mom said. "Homes with people
who can keep them and pay for
their food."

"Oh, OK," said Timmy.

Pete had moved the cat's box
back away from the heater so
Duke's basket was nearer.

"Now time for bed!" Mom said.
Timmy gave Tiger one last hug.

Pete had left the kitchen, so Timmy moved the cat's box back in front of the heater. "Sleep well," he said to him.

# 6. Tiger, the Star

Timmy stayed up for a long time. He wanted to think of ways to make money so he could keep Tiger.

He did not want Tiger down at the animal shelter lost and alone. Tiger was his.

He had to be his!

Timmy tossed and turned, but he still could not think of a way out, so he fell asleep.

The clock in the hall downstairs had just chimed three when he suddenly woke up again. For a while he just lay there, and then he knew that there was something licking his ear. Something wet. It was Tiger licking him!

"What are you doing here?" Timmy said.

Tiger licked Timmy's ear all over.

Timmy was about to drift back
to sleep when Tiger started
meowing loudly.
Meow...MEOW...MEOW!

"What's the matter?" Timmy said. "What do you want?"

Tiger meowed even more, so Timmy put on the lamp.

And then he smelled it. Smoke!

Timmy gasped, ran to the door, and looked down the hall. Smoke was coming from under the living room door and coming up the stairs. He could hear a noise from the living room—a scary, crackling, burning noise.

Timmy grabbed Tiger. "FIRE!"
he yelled at the top of his lungs.
"Mom! Pete!" He ran to their
doors. "Fire! Get out quickly!"

● ● ●

"So this is the hero, is it?" said the fireman, clapping Timmy on the back.

It was a bit later. Everyone was safe. The fire was out.

"Yes, it was Timmy who woke us all up," Mom said.

Timmy said, "No, it was not me. It was Tiger, my cat."

"What?!" said Mom.

"Really?" said Pete.

"Is that right?" said the fireman.

"He woke me up. He came on the bed and licked my ear. Then he meowed loudly. He's the hero...." Timmy picked up Tiger. "Can I keep him now, Mom?"

Mom smiled. "Well, yes, you can," she said. "We will find a way."

"I'll get him a basket," Pete
said. "It can be next to Duke's
basket in the kitchen."

"I'll get his story in the local
paper!" the fireman said. "Brave
cat saves family!"

"Hear that?" Timmy said to Tiger. "You are going to be a star!"